By Brandon T Mayes

Joann and Jane: Who Made This Mess?
Penguins Don't Live in the Fridge
Joann and Jane: Where's London Dog?
The Economic Symphony

The Economic
Symphony

The Economic Symphony

The Economic

Symphony

A Story of Markets, Music,
and Making Change

Brandon T Mayes

The Economic Symphony: A Story of Markets, Music, and
Making Change

ISBN: 978-1-953515-29-2 (Hardcover)
ISBN: 978-1-953515-30-8 (Paperback)
ISBN: 978-1-953515-31-5 (E-Book)

First Edition

For my children, may you change the world.

For my students, understand that the world is always changing, and you can affect that change.

The Economic Symphony

Chapter 1: The Interview

Maya Chen wiped her sweaty palms on her charcoal pencil skirt before pressing the elevator button for the 42nd floor of Renaissance Tower. At seventeen, she was probably the youngest person ever to interview for an internship at Nexus Analytics, one of Dallas's fastest-growing financial technology companies. But then again, most high school juniors didn't spend their free time creating algorithms to predict cryptocurrency price fluctuations.

The elevator doors opened directly into Nexus's lobby, all sleek glass and brushed steel. A massive digital display showed real-time market data streaming across multiple screens — the S&P 500 was down 2.3%, the Dow had dropped 600 points, and Bitcoin was experiencing what the crypto bros called "a healthy correction" (which Maya knew really meant "panic selling").

"Miss Chen?" The receptionist's voice cut through her market analysis. "Ms. Rodriguez will see you now."

Maya followed the receptionist down a corridor lined with empty offices. The post-pandemic hybrid work model meant that only about a third of Nexus's employees came into the office on any given day. Her economics teacher, Mr. Washington, had spent an entire class discussing how remote work was reshaping the commercial real estate market in downtown Dallas.

"Have a seat," said Carmen Rodriguez, Nexus's Chief Operating Officer, gesturing to a chair across from her standing desk. She remained standing, her dark eyes scanning Maya's resume. "So, you developed a trading algorithm that outperformed the S&P 500 by 12% over six months?"

Maya sat up straighter. "Yes, ma'am. I used machine learning to analyze patterns in market sentiment from social media posts, combined with traditional technical indicators and—"

"And you didn't actually trade with it?" Ms. Rodriguez interrupted.

"No, ma'am. Paper trading only. SEC regulations prohibit anyone under eighteen from opening their own brokerage account." Maya had researched all the relevant securities laws. "But I documented all the theoretical trades and calculated the returns accounting for spreads and transaction costs."

Ms. Rodriguez's expression softened slightly. "Good answer. Too many young people these days think they can get rich quick by day trading GameStop options." She finally sat down. "Tell me, Maya, why do you want this internship?"

Maya had rehearsed her answer to this question dozens of times, but now she decided to tell the truth instead. "Because I want to understand how money really works. Not just the theoretical supply and demand curves we learn about in AP Econ, but how real markets function. How rational and irrational human behavior shapes the economy. How technology is changing everything." She paused. "And because I want to make sure that whatever happens with the economy, my family will be okay."

That last part had slipped out unintentionally. Maya thought about her parents' restaurant, how they'd barely survived the pandemic, and how rising food costs were now squeezing their margins to almost nothing. She thought about the student loans she'd need for college, and how much they tried to avoid getting into debt.

Ms. Rodriguez studied her for a long moment. "The markets are brutal, Maya. They don't care about your family or your dreams. They'll chew you up and spit you out if you let them." She leaned forward. "But if you're smart – and your resume suggests you are – you can learn to navigate them. Maybe even help others do the same."

She stood up and extended her hand. "The internship is yours if you want it. Three months, twenty hours per week, paid of course. We'll work around your school schedule."

Maya stood too, trying to keep her hand steady as she shook Ms. Rodriguez's. "Thank you, I won't let you down."

"I know you won't." Ms. Rodriguez smiled for the first time. "Because if that trading algorithm of yours is half as good as you claim, we might just have to acquire it. Welcome to Nexus Analytics, Maya. Your real education is about to begin."

As Maya rode the elevator back down to street level, her mind was already racing with possibilities. She had a foot in the door. Now she just had to figure out how to open it wider – not just for herself, but for everyone who was counting on her.

Her phone buzzed with a text from her best friend Zoe: "How did it go???"

Maya smiled as she typed her reply: "I got it. But that's just the beginning."

She stepped out into the hot Texas sunshine, looking up at the Dallas skyline stretching above her. Somewhere in those gleaming towers, fortunes were being made and lost every second. Maya Chen intended to learn exactly how and why.

And then she intended to change the game entirely.

Chapter 2: First Day

Maya arrived at Nexus Analytics early, her laptop bag slung over one shoulder and a travel mug of her mom's Vietnamese coffee in her hand. The security guard, an older man named Earl, greeted her with a warm smile as he handed over her freshly printed ID badge.

"First day jitters?" he asked, noticing her fingers drumming against the coffee mug.

"That obvious, huh?"

"Everyone's got 'em. Even Ms. Rodriguez did on her first day, and that was back when we were just a startup on the third floor." He winked. "You'll do fine."

The morning orientation flew by in a blur of paperwork, security protocols, and IT setup. By lunch, Maya's head was spinning with more acronyms than she'd ever encountered in her AP classes. But things got interesting when she finally met her supervisor, a quantitative analyst named Marcus Wells.

"So you're the high school wunderkind," Marcus said, leading her to a desk in the open office area. "Let's see what you've got. Pull up your trading algorithm."

Maya opened her laptop and walked him through her code. She'd built it using Python, pulling data from multiple sources to analyze market trends. Marcus nodded approvingly at her comments and documentation.

"Not bad at all. But see this part here?" He pointed to a section of her code. "You're not accounting for market liquidity. In theory, your trades would work. In practice, you'd get killed by slippage."

Maya frowned. "Slippage?"

"The difference between the expected price of a trade and its actual execution price. It's like..." Marcus paused, thinking. "You know how gas prices can vary by fifty cents between stations just a few miles apart?"

"Yeah, drives my dad crazy. He uses an app to find the cheapest gas in town."

"Exactly. Now imagine if everyone used that app and rushed to the cheapest station. What would happen?"

Maya thought about it. "The station would run out of gas. And people at the back of the line would either have to wait or go somewhere else."

"Bingo. That's basically what happens in the market when too many people try to execute the same trade at once. The price moves against you. Big institutional investors deal with this all the time – it's why they break up large orders into smaller chunks."

Maya started taking notes. This was the kind of real-world knowledge she couldn't get from textbooks.

"Your next project," Marcus continued, "is to help me analyze some market inefficiencies we've noticed in the renewable energy sector. But first, lunch? The team usually orders from different local places and eats together in the break room. Today's Thai food."

Over lunch, Maya met more of her colleagues. There was Sarah from compliance, who used to work for the SEC; Dev from IT, who could write code faster than anyone Maya had ever seen; and James from research, who was working on using satellite imagery to predict agricultural commodity prices.

The conversation turned to the morning's market news — the Federal Reserve was hinting at another interest rate hike.

"There goes the housing market," Sarah sighed. "My sister's been trying to buy her first home, but with rates this high..."

"Yeah, but inflation's still running hot," James countered. "Fed's got to do something."

Maya listened intently, connecting the dots between their discussion and what she'd learned in Mr. Washington's class about monetary policy. It was fascinating seeing how these big economic decisions filtered down to affect real people – from homebuyers to small business owners like her parents.

After lunch, Maya dove into the renewable energy project. Marcus had given her access to a massive dataset tracking solar panel installation rates across different states, along with energy prices, tax incentives, and weather patterns.

"Look for correlations," he'd said. "But remember — correlation isn't causation. We need to understand the real drivers behind adoption rates."

By the end of the day, Maya's brain was exhausted but buzzing with new ideas. As she packed up her laptop, Ms. Rodriguez stopped by her desk.

"How was day one?"

"Amazing," Maya replied honestly. "I learned more today than in a month of regular classes."

Ms. Rodriguez nodded. "That's because here, it's not just theory. It's real money, real consequences." She paused. "Speaking of which, how's your family's restaurant doing with the inflation situation?"

Maya was surprised she remembered that detail from their interview. "It's... challenging. Food costs keep rising, but they can't raise prices too much or they'll lose customers."

"Classic price elasticity problem," Ms. Rodriguez mused. "Tell you what – why don't you apply some of what you're learning here to analyze their business model? Maybe we can help them find some solutions."

Maya's eyes widened. "Really? That would be incredible!"

"Just remember our confidentiality agreement," Ms. Rodriguez smiled. "No sharing proprietary trading strategies. But general business analysis? That's fair game."

As Maya headed home on the DART train, she pulled out her notebook and started sketching ideas. Supply chains, price points, operating costs – she could apply the same analytical approach she used for market data to her family's business.

Her phone buzzed with a text from her mom: "How was first day? Did you eat lunch?"

Maya smiled as she typed back: "Best day ever. And mom... I think I might have some ideas to help with the restaurant."

Looking out the train window at the Dallas sunset, Maya felt a surge of purpose. She wasn't just here to learn about money – she was here to learn how to make it work better for everyone.

Chapter 3: Data Mining

"Mom, can I see the restaurant's books?"

Maya's mother looked up from chopping lemongrass, her knife pausing mid-slice. It was Sunday morning, and Maya had come to Phở Ngon early to help prep for the lunch rush. The restaurant's small kitchen was already thick with the aromatic steam of simmering beef bones.

"The books?" Her mother's forehead creased. "Why?"

"I want to help." Maya pulled out her laptop. "At Nexus, we analyze data to find patterns and solve problems. Maybe I can do the same thing here."

Her mother wiped her hands on her apron and sat down at the small prep table. "Your father and I have been running restaurants for twenty years. Since before you were born. What can a computer tell us that we don't already know?"

Maya opened a spreadsheet. "Let me show you. What if we could predict exactly how many people will come each day? How much phở to prep? When to order supplies? It could help reduce waste and save money."

Her mother was quiet for a moment, then stood up and went to the office. She returned with a stack of papers – receipts, invoices, and the daily sales records she meticulously kept by hand.

"Here. But Maya?" She touched her daughter's cheek. "Don't worry so much. We will survive, like we always have."

"I know, Mom. But maybe we can do more than survive."

Maya spent the morning entering three months of data into her laptop, creating neat columns of numbers: daily sales, ingredient costs, labor hours, even weather conditions. Between helping with prep work, she began to see patterns emerging.

Her phone buzzed with a text from Marcus: "Check your email. Need your eyes on something."

Maya opened her work email to find a cryptic message:

```

Found anomaly in renewable energy data. Multiple suppliers reporting unexpected inventory surpluses. Market's not pricing this correctly. Dig deeper?
```

She glanced at her mother's records, then back at the email. Something clicked.

"Mom, when did food costs start rising the most?"

"March. Every delivery, higher prices. Mr. Lee at the Asian market said something about shipping containers, fuel costs..."

Maya nodded, pulling up shipping rate data on her laptop. Global supply chain disruptions were causing ripple effects everywhere – from restaurant supplies to solar panels.

Her phone buzzed again. This time it was Zoe: "Still on for study group? AP Econ test tomorrow!"

Maya had almost forgotten. She looked at the half-analyzed restaurant data, then at her mother, who was now expertly assembling spring rolls.

"Go," her mother said, reading her expression. "Study is important. The restaurant will be here."

"Thanks, Mom. But first..." Maya quickly created a pivot table from the morning's data entry. "Look at this. Our busiest days aren't actually weekends — they're rainy weekdays. And the profit margin on bánh mì is actually higher than phở, even though we sell less."

Her mother leaned in, squinting at the screen. "How can you tell all this from numbers?"

"The data tells a story, Mom. Just like how you can taste the broth and know exactly what it needs." Maya pointed to a graph. "See this line? It shows how many customers we get based on weather and day of the week. We could use this to plan better, maybe run specials on slow days."

For the first time, her mother looked genuinely interested. "Show me more tonight?"

"Promise." Maya packed up her laptop. "And Mom? Thanks for trusting me with the books."

At the study group in Zoe's kitchen, Maya's mind kept drifting between her AP Econ review, the restaurant data, and Marcus's email about the renewable energy anomaly. As Zoe quizzed them on aggregate supply curves, Maya suddenly sat up straight.

"Maya? You okay?" Zoe asked.

"Yeah, just... thinking. You know how Mr. Washington talked about how changes in one market can affect other markets?"

"Sure," said Tommy, another study group member. "Like how gas prices affect food prices because of transportation costs."

"Right. But what if we could predict those effects? See them coming before they hit?" Maya opened her laptop and pulled up both sets of data – the restaurant's numbers and Nexus's renewable energy metrics.

She began sketching in her notebook: supply chains, price trajectories, interconnected markets. The solar panel surplus could be a leading indicator of wider market shifts. And if small businesses like her family's restaurant were feeling the squeeze now...

"Maya?" Zoe waved a hand in front of her face. "Earth to Maya? We're on fiscal policy now."

"Sorry." Maya blinked, returning to the study guide. But her mind was racing with possibilities. Tomorrow, she'd show Marcus what she'd found. There was a bigger picture here, and she was starting to see it.

That night, after closing, Maya sat with her parents at one of the restaurant's tables, her laptop open between bowls of leftover phở.

"If we adjust the menu prices seasonally," she explained, "and change our ordering pattern based on these demand predictions..." She walked them through her analysis, translating the graphs and numbers into practical steps they could take.

Her father, who had been quiet until now, spoke up. "You learned all this in one week at your internship?"

"I learned the tools there," Maya said. "But I learned about hard work and adaptation from you and Mom." She turned to a new spreadsheet. "Now, let me show you what we could do with online ordering and analytics..."

Her parents exchanged a look – the same one they'd had when she'd first shown them her trading algorithm. A mixture of pride, worry, and cautious hope.

Outside, the Dallas night was alive with traffic and possibility. Tomorrow would bring a calculus test, more market data to analyze, and endless restaurant tasks. But for now, Maya felt the pieces of her world starting to align – numbers and noodles, algorithms and family recipes, all coming together in ways she was only beginning to understand.

She just hoped she was right about the patterns she was seeing. Because if she was, big changes were coming to more than just her family's restaurant.

Chapter 4: Unexpected Harmonies

Maya's fingers flew across her laptop keyboard in the school library during lunch period, trying to finish her analysis before orchestra practice. The renewable energy data was starting to show a fascinating pattern, but she couldn't quite grasp its full implications yet.

"There you are!" Zoe dropped into the chair beside her, carefully setting her French horn case under the table. "You missed the whole drama at morning band practice. Mr. Peterson nearly had a meltdown about the spring concert budget."

"What happened?" Maya asked, half listening as she tweaked her Python script.

"Remember how the school board increased funding for arts programs?" Zoe pulled out her lunch. "Turns out it's getting eaten up by inflation. The new sheet music prices are insane, and don't even get me started on instrument repair costs."

Maya's head snapped up. "Wait, what?"

"Yeah, everything's getting more expensive. Even my horn's valve oil went up two dollars." Zoe paused, noting Maya's intense expression. "Why are you looking at me like I just solved a calculus problem?"

Before Maya could answer, Tommy hurried over, still wearing his theater department t-shirt from morning rehearsal. "Maya! Need your economic brain. Our spring musical is in trouble."

"Let me guess," Maya said slowly. "Budget issues?"

"How'd you know? We picked 'Rent' because it has minimal set requirements, but even the basics – lumber, paint, lighting gels – they're all—"

"More expensive than expected," Maya finished. She turned her laptop so they could see the charts on her screen. "Look at this. I've been tracking price increases across different sectors for my internship. See this spike in raw materials and shipping costs? It's not just hitting one industry – it's cascading through everything."

"Like dominoes?" Tommy asked, leaning in.

"More like..." Maya thought for a moment. "More like ripples in a pond. Or maybe..." She glanced at Zoe's French horn. "Like harmonics. You know how when you play one note, it affects other strings through sympathetic vibration?"

Zoe's eyes lit up. "That's actually a perfect metaphor. In orchestra, every instrument's part affects the overall piece. Change one thing, and it impacts everything else."

"Exactly!" Maya opened a new tab in her spreadsheet. "The solar panel surplus I've been investigating at work – it's not just about renewable energy. It's connected to these supply chain disruptions, which affect shipping costs, which impact everything from your valve oil to Tommy's set materials to my parents' restaurant supplies."

"Speaking of the musical," Tommy said, checking his phone, "I need to get to rehearsal. Ms. Martinez is drilling choreography today, and you know how she gets when people are late."

"And I need to practice for All-State auditions," Zoe added. "But Maya, this is fascinating. Can we talk more at study group?"

Maya nodded, already typing furiously. "Actually, can we move study group to the orchestra room today? I want to try something."

Later that afternoon, Maya spread her materials across the orchestra room's piano while her friends unpacked their instruments for afternoon practice. The band kids had already cleared out, leaving just the orchestra students tuning up.

"Okay," Maya said, pointing to her laptop screen. "Look at these market patterns. They're cyclical, with smaller fluctuations building into larger trends. Kind of like..."

She turned to Jessica, the first-chair violinist who had joined their study group. "Jess, can you play a simple melody? Something with clear rhythm?"

Jessica raised her violin and played a few bars of a classical piece, the familiar tune floating through the room.

"Now," Maya said, "Zoe, can you add your part?"

Zoe joined in with her French horn, adding harmonic depth to the melody.

"See how they work together? Now imagine each instrument represents a different market sector." Maya pulled up another graph. "When one part changes rhythm or volume, the others have to adjust to stay in harmony. The economy works the same way."

"So the solar panel surplus..." Tommy began, looking up from highlighting his script.

"Is like a key change in the middle of a piece," Maya finished. "It signals a bigger shift coming. The question is — what's driving the change, and how do we adapt to it?"

She glanced at her phone — she had a text from Marcus about tomorrow's meeting at Nexus. They wanted her initial findings on the renewable energy analysis.

"Maya Chen," Zoe said, lowering her French horn, "I think you just turned the economy into a symphony."

"Maybe I did." Maya smiled, screenshotting her charts. "And maybe that's exactly how I need to explain it to my boss tomorrow."

The orchestra began warming up in earnest now, the cacophony of individual instruments slowly tuning and aligning. Maya packed up her laptop, pausing to listen as the disparate sounds merged into harmony.

That's what she needed to show Marcus and Ms. Rodriguez — not just the individual data points, but how they all played together in the larger economic composition. And maybe, just maybe, she could help her parents' restaurant find its place in that symphony too.

As she headed out, she heard Tommy practicing his lines for the musical. The words seemed oddly appropriate for her economic research. In markets, as in music, everything was connected. The trick was learning to hear the connections.

Her phone buzzed with a text from her mother: "Big delivery came in. Prices higher again. Still coming to help prep tomorrow morning?"

"Be there at 6," Maya typed back. "And Mom? I think I'm starting to understand something important about these price changes. Will explain tomorrow."

She walked through the school hallway, past the theater where the musical set was half-built, past the band room where the budget papers still sat on Mr. Peterson's desk, her mind weaving together markets and music, supply chains and symphonies.

Tomorrow would be interesting, both at Nexus and at the restaurant. But for now, she had one more AP Econ chapter to review – appropriately enough, it was about market interconnectedness and economic indicators.

Sometimes, Maya thought, the best way to understand complex systems was to find the right metaphor. And thanks to her friends, she might have just found one that could change everything.

Chapter 5: The Presentation

Maya arrived at Nexus Analytics early, her presentation ready on her laptop. She'd stayed up late refining her analysis, fueled by her mother's coffee and the excitement of discovery. The office was quiet – most employees wouldn't arrive for another hour – but Marcus was already at his desk.

"Ready for the morning briefing?" he asked, glancing up from his monitors.

"I think so. But I'm taking a slightly... different approach."

Marcus raised an eyebrow. "Different how?"

Before Maya could answer, her phone buzzed. It was Jessica from orchestra: "Break a leg! Remember - dynamics make the performance. Also, can you still help me with AP Econ homework later?"

The message reminded Maya of something. She quickly opened her laptop. "Actually, Marcus, could we use the conference room with the good speakers?"

Thirty minutes later, Maya stood before Ms. Rodriguez, Marcus, and several other team members in the glass-walled conference room. Her hands were steady as she pulled up her first slide.

"We've been looking at the renewable energy market anomaly the wrong way," she began. "We've been focused on the solar panel surplus in isolation, but it's actually part of a larger pattern." She clicked to the next slide, showing multiple overlapping graphs.

"These look like wave patterns," Sarah from compliance noted.

"Exactly." Maya smiled. "Because markets move like music." She pressed play on her laptop, and a simple violin melody filled the room – Jessica had helped her record it last night.

"This is the solar panel market over the past year." Another click added a French horn line. "And this is shipping container rates." A cello entered the melody. "Raw material costs." Finally, a bass line. "Oil prices."

The music built into a complex harmony, then began to shift into a minor key.

"Hear how the parts interact? When one changes, the others adjust. Just like in an orchestra, just like in the economy." Maya switched to her data visualization. "The solar panel surplus isn't the problem – it's an early warning. A leading indicator."

She walked them through her analysis: how supply chain disruptions were creating cascading effects across multiple industries, how the patterns suggested a larger shift coming in the market. She used her family's restaurant's challenges as a micro-level example, then zoomed out to show the macro implications.

When she finished, the room was quiet except for the final notes of the musical piece fading away.

Ms. Rodriguez leaned forward. "You're suggesting we adjust our entire renewable energy investment strategy based on... restaurant supplies and orchestra music?"

Maya took a deep breath. "I'm suggesting we look at market patterns the way we look at musical patterns. Everything's connected. The key is finding the underlying rhythm."

Marcus was nodding slowly. "The correlation matrices support her analysis. And if she's right about these leading indicators..."

"We could position ourselves ahead of the market shift," Ms. Rodriguez finished. She studied Maya for a moment. "How did you spot this pattern?"

"My friends, actually. Band budget issues, theater supply costs – it helped me see the connections. Sometimes you need to step back to see how all the pieces fit together."

"Like a conductor's view of the orchestra," Ms. Rodriguez mused. She stood up. "Develop this further. I want a detailed implementation strategy by next week. And Maya?" She paused at the door. "Nice work thinking outside the box."

After the meeting, Maya's phone lit up with texts from her study group:

Zoe: "Coming to band practice? Mr. Peterson wants to discuss fundraising ideas."

Tommy: "Theater crew found cheaper lumber source. Your supplier research helped!"

Jessica: "Still need Econ help. But can we talk about your market-music theory too?"

Maya smiled as she typed her replies. Then she opened a new document and began outlining her implementation strategy. But this time, she included a section on small business applications. What she was learning at Nexus could help more than just big investors.

That evening at Phở Ngon, Maya showed her parents a simplified version of her analysis.

"See these patterns?" She pointed to her laptop screen. "They show us when to expect price changes. We can adjust our ordering and menu pricing ahead of time."

Her father frowned at the graphs. "But how can we know it's accurate?"

"Remember last month when bean sprout prices suddenly jumped? That coincided with this pattern here." Maya highlighted a section. "If we watch these indicators, we can prepare better."

Her mother set down a bowl of phở beside Maya's laptop. "Like knowing when to buy extra ingredients before Tết festival?"

"Exactly! It's about anticipating demand and price changes." Maya took a sip of the broth – perfect as always. "And I have some ideas about our menu pricing too."

She explained how they could use dynamic pricing – charging slightly different prices at different times based on demand patterns, just like how concert ticket prices varied by seat and show time.

"Not big changes," she assured them, seeing their concerned looks. "Just small adjustments to help cover the rising costs without losing customers. And look – we can offer special deals during traditionally slow times to bring in more business."

Her father was quiet for a moment, then said, "Your old father never thought he'd be taking business advice from his teenage daughter." He smiled. "But these are not normal times. And you're not a normal teenager."

"I learned from the best," Maya said, hugging them both. "You taught me about hard work and adaptation. I'm just adding some new tools."

Later that night, as she worked on her AP Econ homework with Jessica over video chat, Maya reflected on how much her worlds had started to overlap – music and markets, family and finance, school and real-world applications.

"Hey Maya," Jessica said, looking up from her supply and demand curves, "you know what your market theory reminds me of? Tchaikovsky's Fourth Symphony. It's all about fate and how everything's connected."

Maya made a note to look up the symphony. She had a feeling it might inspire her next analysis.

Her phone buzzed with an email from Ms. Rodriguez: "Meeting with potential investors next month. Would like you to present your findings. Keep developing the musical metaphor – you might be onto something important."

Maya looked at her window at the Dallas skyline, the office buildings lit up like stars. Somewhere out there, markets were moving to their own rhythm. She was learning to hear the music – and maybe, just maybe, she could help others hear it too.

First, though, she had to finish her AP Econ homework. Tomorrow would bring another day of balancing school, work, and family. But for the first time, it all felt like part of the same symphony.

Chapter 6: The Ripple Effect

"What do you mean we might have to cancel the spring musical?" Tommy's voice cracked with disbelief. The theater kids had gathered in their usual corner of the cafeteria, scripts and set design sketches scattered across the table.

Maya looked up from her investor presentation draft. She'd been using her lunch periods to work on it, but this was more important. "Walk me through the numbers."

Ms. Martinez, the theater director, had given Tommy a breakdown of their budget crisis. Between rising material costs and lower ticket sales from previous shows, they were looking at a significant shortfall.

"We've already switched to 'Rent' because it needs minimal sets," Tommy explained, pushing his sketchbook toward Maya. "But even with that..."

Maya studied the budget figures while taking a bite of her mom's bánh mì. Even simple materials like plywood and paint had jumped nearly 40% in price. Her analysis at Nexus had predicted these increases, but seeing their impact on her friends made it personal.

Zoe slid into the seat beside them, French horn case in tow. "Any solution yet? Because band's having similar issues. Mr. Peterson's talking about cutting the spring concert series down to one show instead of three."

Maya pulled out her laptop, opening a new spreadsheet. "Okay, let's think about this systematically. What are your main revenue sources?"

"Ticket sales, concessions, program ads..." Tommy listed.

"And what about cross-promotion?" Maya asked, her fingers flying across the keyboard.

"What do you mean?"

"Well, look at it like market synergy." Maya turned her laptop to show them. "The theater department needs funds. The band needs performance opportunities. What if we combined resources?"

Zoe leaned in. "Like having the band play before shows? We could do a mini-concert in the lobby..."

"Exactly! And" – Maya pulled up another document – "remember how my parents' restaurant improved profits by adjusting prices based on demand? We could apply the same principle to ticket sales."

She explained her idea: early-bird discounts to guarantee initial sales, premium pricing for optimal show dates, special package deals combining theater tickets with band performances. They could even sell advertising spots in both theater programs and band concert booklets to maximize revenue.

"It's like what we learned in AP Econ about economies of scale," Jessica added, joining them with her violin case. "By combining resources, we reduce overhead costs per event."

Maya nodded enthusiastically. "And create new value through collaboration. Here, look at these projections..."

She walked them through the numbers, translating market principles into practical solutions. By the end of lunch, they had a workable plan to present to Ms. Martinez and Mr. Peterson.

"Maya," Tommy said, staring at the spreadsheet, "you're kind of a genius."

"Nah, just good at seeing patterns." She started packing up. "Speaking of which, I need to get to my internship. But text me after you talk to Ms. Martinez?"

At Nexus that afternoon, Maya was deep in preparation for her investor presentation when Marcus stopped by her desk.

"How's it coming along?"

"Actually..." Maya pulled up her work. "I've been thinking about adding a new component. The solar panel surplus isn't just affecting big markets — it's having downstream effects on small businesses and community organizations. I've been seeing it firsthand."

She showed him how she'd expanded her analysis to include examples from various economic levels — from global supply chains down to local theater productions.

"The investors might appreciate that," Marcus mused. "It shows real-world applications. But keep the musical metaphor. It's unique."

31

Maya's phone buzzed — a series of excited texts from Tommy and Zoe. Both teachers had approved their plan. The spring musical and band concert series were saved, pending final budget committee approval.

"Speaking of applications," Maya said, "remember how we discussed market inefficiencies last week? I think I've found some interesting parallels in community-level economics."

She explained how small organizations often struggled with the same market forces as large corporations, just on a different scale. Her friends' experiences had helped her see how economic principles played out across all levels.

"You're developing quite a holistic view of market dynamics," Marcus observed.

"I have to. My parents' restaurant, my friends' activities — they're all connected to these bigger economic patterns we're tracking. Understanding one helps me understand the other."

That evening, Maya sat in on the orchestra's rehearsal, laptop open as she refined her investor presentation. The music washed over her as she worked — Tchaikovsky's Fourth Symphony, the piece Jessica had mentioned.

As the different sections of the orchestra came together, Maya thought about how markets worked the same way. Individual players and instruments, each following their own part, created something larger than themselves. Just like how her family's restaurant, her friends' school activities, and the global markets she studied at Nexus were all part of a larger economic symphony.

Her phone lit up with a message from Ms. Rodriguez: "Board wants preliminary look at your presentation next month. Would like you to present your findings. Keep developing the musical metaphor – you might be onto something important."

Maya looked at her screen, then at her friends in the orchestra. She thought about Tommy's theater group and Zoe's band, about her parents' restaurant and the patterns she'd discovered at Nexus. Everything was connected, and she was finally learning to see – and hear – those connections.

"Ready," she typed back. Because understanding economics wasn't just about charts and numbers. It was about seeing how every part of the economy, from the smallest purchase to the largest market trend, played its role in the greater composition.

The orchestra swelled into the symphony's final movement. Maya saved her presentation and closed her laptop, letting the music wash over her. Tomorrow she'd show the board how all these pieces fit together. But for now, she was just a teenager doing homework in her family's restaurant, surrounded by the community she'd helped bring together.

And for once, that felt like exactly enough.

Chapter 7: Symphony in Supply and Demand

Maya stood in the Nexus conference room bathroom, adjusting her blazer – a loan from Zoe's older sister. Her morning had started at 5 AM helping her parents with restaurant prep, followed by a quick AP Calc quiz, and now this: presenting to the Nexus board and potential investors.

Her phone buzzed with encouraging messages:

Zoe: "You've got this! Just like conducting the band 🎶"
Tommy: "Break a leg! (theater kid approved)"
Jessica: "Remember - breathe between movements 🎻"
Mom: "Con gái của mẹ là ngôi sao sáng" (My daughter is a bright star)

Taking a deep breath, Maya headed to the conference room. The Dallas skyline stretched behind the floor-to-ceiling windows, and around the massive table sat the Nexus board members, three potential investors, and – Maya's heart jumped – a representative from Goldman Sachs.

Ms. Rodriguez nodded encouragingly. "Maya, whenever you're ready."

Maya connected her laptop to the display. "Thank you for having me. Today, I'd like to show you how understanding market patterns is similar to understanding music – and why that matters for our investment strategy."

She launched her presentation, starting with the same musical piece she'd used before, but now enhanced with professional audio equipment. The violin's opening notes filled the room.

"This melody represents the solar panel market over the past year." She highlighted corresponding data points on her chart. "Notice the rhythm, the pattern. Now, listen as we add more elements."

Layer by layer, she built up the market symphony she'd created, each instrument representing a different economic sector. But this time, she'd added something new — a subtle discord in the harmony.

"Hear that tension? It's not just in the music. Look at these market indicators." She switched to a complex data visualization. "The solar panel surplus isn't an isolated anomaly. It's part of a larger pattern of supply chain disruptions and market adjustments."

Maya walked them through her analysis, using examples from global markets down to local businesses. She explained how studying small-scale economic impacts had helped her identify larger trends.

"When an orchestra plays, every instrument affects every other instrument. Markets work the same way. What happens in renewable energy affects shipping costs, which affects small businesses, which affects consumer spending, which cycles back to impact larger markets."

The Goldman Sachs representative leaned forward. "You're suggesting these micro-level indicators could predict macro-level market shifts?"

"Yes, but more importantly—" Maya clicked to her next slide, revealing a new pattern she'd discovered last night. "They're showing us something now."

The room grew silent as she explained what she'd found: early signs of a potential market correction, visible first in small-business data but now appearing in larger market indicators.

"The good news is, we have time to prepare. The same patterns showing us the problem also show us opportunities." She outlined her recommended strategy, including ways to protect current investments while positioning for future growth.

When she finished, there was a moment of quiet, broken by an unexpected sound – applause, started by Ms. Rodriguez and quickly spreading around the table.

The questions came rapid-fire after that. Maya handled them confidently, drawing on everything from her AP Econ knowledge to her family's restaurant experience to her friends' school activities to support her points.

"One last question," the Goldman Sachs representative said. "What made you think to look at small-business indicators?"

Maya thought about her parents' restaurant, about Tommy's theater budget and Zoe's band fundraising. "Because that's where you feel market changes first. Like how musicians in an orchestra feel rhythm changes before the audience hears them."

After the meeting, Ms. Rodriguez pulled Maya aside. "The board is impressed. Very impressed. They want to expand your analysis into a full market research project."

Maya's eyes widened. "Really?"

"With compensation to match. And Goldman Sachs expressed interest in our findings." Ms. Rodriguez smiled. "How does it feel to have major Wall Street firms paying attention to your work?"

"Honestly? A little surreal." Maya checked her phone – she had AP Econ class in an hour. "But exciting."

"Good. Because this is just the beginning. I want you to lead the research team on this project."

"Lead? But I'm just an intern..."

"An intern who just showed us something nobody else noticed." Ms. Rodriguez handed her a folder. "Here's the paperwork for an extended internship through summer. Think about it."

Back at school, Maya slid into her AP Econ class just as Mr. Washington was starting a lesson on market indicators. Her friends shot her questioning looks – they knew about her presentation.

"Today we're discussing leading and lagging indicators," Mr. Washington began. "Can anyone give us an example?"

Maya smiled to herself as she raised her hand. She had a few examples to share.

Later, at lunch, she told her friends about the presentation's success while they worked on their respective projects – Tommy reviewing set design budgets, Zoe organizing band fundraiser details, Jessica marking up orchestra scores.

"So you're basically a Wall Street genius now?" Tommy teased.

"Hardly." Maya pulled out her laptop. "But speaking of budgets, I had some new ideas for the theater fundraising..."

She'd realized something important during her presentation: success wasn't just about seeing patterns – it was about using that knowledge to help others. Whether it was global markets or school activities, economics was really about understanding connections and making things work better for everyone.

Her phone buzzed with a text from her mother: "Big supplier meeting tomorrow. Can you bring your numbers?"

"Of course," Maya replied. She had a feeling her next big challenge would be helping her parents negotiate better supply contracts using her new market insights.

The final bell rang, and Maya packed up her things, heading to orchestra practice. She had a lot to think about – the extended internship offer, the research project, her parents' restaurant, her friends' activities. But somehow, it all felt right, like different instruments coming together in perfect harmony.

As she walked through the halls of her high school, Maya Chen – intern, daughter, friend, and now recognized market analyst – smiled. She was learning to hear the music of markets, and better yet, learning to help others hear it too.

The symphony was just beginning.

Chapter 8: Crescendo

"Your daughter tells us we should expect another price increase in six weeks," Mr. Lee said in Vietnamese, looking at Maya's parents across his office desk. They were in the back room of the Asian grocery supply store that had provided ingredients to Phở Ngon for over a decade.

Maya sat quietly beside her parents, laptop open to her market analysis. She'd asked to come along to their supplier meeting, and now she watched as Mr. Lee studied her charts.

"How can she know this?" he asked.

Maya's father glanced at her, nodding encouragingly. She pulled up another graph. "These shipping container rates from Asia show a clear pattern," she explained in Vietnamese, pointing to the trend lines. "When they rise like this, we typically see wholesale price increases six to eight weeks later."

Mr. Lee leaned forward, adjusting his reading glasses. "You work at that big company downtown now, yes? In the tall building?"

Maya nodded. "I analyze market patterns. And the patterns say we should lock in prices now, before the increase." She turned to a new spreadsheet. "I can show you the historical data..."

Two hours later, they walked out with a six-month contract at fixed prices for their most important ingredients. Maya's mother squeezed her hand. "Your father and I never thought to ask for a long-term contract before."

"Most small businesses don't," Maya said. "But with market volatility increasing—" She stopped, seeing her mother's amused expression. "Sorry. I'm starting to sound like my bosses."

"No," her mother smiled. "You sound like yourself. Just... growing."

Maya's phone buzzed – a reminder about the research team meeting at Nexus in an hour. Then another text from Tommy: "EMERGENCY theater budget meeting after school. Need your brain!"

She looked at her parents. "I have to go to work, but I'll be home for dinner service."

"Go," her father said proudly. "Your mother and I can handle lunch rush. We did manage twenty years without our daughter the economics expert," he teased.

At Nexus, Maya led her first research team meeting. It felt surreal having analysts twice her age taking notes as she explained her methodology.

"The key is looking at unconventional indicators," she explained, showing how she'd mapped small business data against larger market trends. "Traditional metrics might miss early warning signs that are visible at the local level."

"Like canaries in a coal mine," Marcus added from his seat by the window.

"Exactly. Or like how you can feel a rhythm change coming in music before you actually hear it." Maya pulled up a new visualization. "Speaking of which, I've identified another pattern we should watch..."

After work, Maya rushed to the theater budget meeting. She found Tommy and Ms. Martinez staring dejectedly at a spreadsheet.

"The lumber supplier backed out," Tommy explained. "Said they can't honor their original quote due to 'market conditions.'"

Maya dropped into a chair, pulling out her laptop. "Let me guess – they're trying to raise prices by at least 30%?"

Ms. Martinez blinked. "How did you know?"

"Because lumber futures are spiking." Maya showed them the charts. "But I might have a solution. Remember how we combined theater and band resources? What if we thought bigger?"

She outlined her idea: partner with other school districts' theater programs to make bulk purchases together.

"If we coordinate with three other schools doing spring musicals, we can leverage economies of scale." She created a quick model. "We'd have enough combined buying power to negotiate better prices, and we could share some resources."

"Like a theater co-op?" Tommy's eyes lit up.

"Exactly! And look—" Maya switched to another tab. "I mapped out potential cost savings. Even after accounting for transportation between schools..."

That evening at Phở Ngon, Maya did her AP Econ homework between helping with dinner service. The restaurant was busy – her parents' new dynamic pricing strategy for the dinner menu was working.

Zoe came in with her French horn case, ordering her usual phở while Maya finished calculating elasticity curves for homework.

"How do you do it all?" Zoe asked, watching Maya bounce between taking orders, running numbers, and solving economics problems.

"Do what?"

"You know – intern at a big finance company, help your parents, save our school activities from budget doom, maintain your GPA..." Zoe slurped her noodles. "Oh, and somehow still make it to orchestra practice."

Maya paused, thinking. "I guess it's because I finally see how it's all connected. Like today – the same market analysis that helped my parents negotiate with their supplier also helped me spot trends at work and figure out solutions for the theater budget."

"There you go again, making economics sound almost interesting," Zoe teased.

"But it is interesting!" Maya protested. "It's like... remember when you taught me about harmonics? How one string vibrating affects others? Economics works the same way. Everything's connected, and once you understand the patterns—"

"You can predict what's coming," Zoe finished. "Like how I can tell you're about to go full econ-nerd on me."

Maya threw a fortune cookie at her friend. "Just wait until tomorrow's AP Econ class. Mr. Washington is covering game theory, and I have some real-world examples to share."

Her phone buzzed – an email from Ms. Rodriguez about an upcoming presentation to more investors. Then a text from Jessica about orchestra practice tomorrow. Then another from her mother asking her to run new numbers for the weekend menu pricing.

Maya looked around the busy restaurant, at Zoe enjoying her phở, at her parents working efficiently in the kitchen, at her homework and market analyses spread across the counter. Different parts of her life, all playing together in unexpected harmony.

She turned back to her elasticity calculations, a new idea forming. Maybe there was a way to quantify the ripple effects of small business decisions on larger markets. She'd have to explore that tomorrow at Nexus.

But for now, she had orders to take, homework to finish, and a friend to stop from stealing her last fortune cookie.

"By the way," Zoe said between bites, "Mr. Peterson wants to know if you can help the band with fundraising strategies next week."

Maya smiled, already pulling up a spreadsheet. "Tell him I've got some ideas."

Because that's what she was learning: economics wasn't just about markets and money. It was about helping people, solving problems, and finding the hidden connections that made everything work better together.

Her phone buzzed again – Tommy sharing exciting news about other schools interested in the theater co-op idea. Maya started typing a response, then stopped to help her mother calculate a bulk order for the weekend.

One thing at a time, she thought. Or maybe many things at once, all playing their parts in the greater symphony.

Chapter 9: Dissonance

Maya stared at her monitor at Nexus, double-checking her calculations. Then triple-checking them. The pattern she'd discovered couldn't be right – but the numbers didn't lie.

"Marcus?" she called across the office. "Can you look at something?"

Her supervisor rolled his chair over, coffee mug in hand. "What's up?"

"Remember how we've been tracking those supply chain disruptions? I think I found something bigger." Maya pulled up her latest analysis. "Look at these correlations."

The data showed an unexpected relationship between the solar panel surplus, shipping rates, and a series of seemingly unrelated market indicators. But when Maya mapped them together...

"This suggests we're not just seeing normal market fluctuations," she explained. "These patterns indicate a fundamental shift in global supply chains. And if I'm right, it's going to hit small businesses first – hard."

Marcus leaned closer, his coffee forgotten. "Walk me through your reasoning."

Maya opened another window showing her family restaurant's supplier data. "See how these local price changes preceded the larger market movements? It's like tremors before an earthquake. And now—" she switched to her latest projections "—I'm seeing the same patterns, but amplified."

"Have you shown this to Ms. Rodriguez?"

"Not yet. I wanted to verify—"

"Show her now," Marcus interrupted. "This could affect our entire investment strategy."

Twenty minutes later, Maya stood in Ms. Rodriguez's office, explaining her findings to both her boss and the Goldman Sachs representative, who had flown in for a portfolio review.

"The supply chain isn't just disrupted," Maya explained. "It's reorganizing. All these small suppliers finding alternative sources, creating new networks – it's changing the entire distribution landscape." She pulled up her visualization, now set to her musical market metaphor. "Listen to how the harmony shifts..."

The familiar market melody played, but now the underlying rhythm was changing, creating new patterns.

"Traditional suppliers are losing their monopolies," Maya continued. "Small businesses are forming buying cooperatives – like what we did with the school theater departments. It's happening everywhere, across different industries."

"This could destabilize existing market structures," the Goldman Sachs representative mused.

"Or create new opportunities," Ms. Rodriguez countered. She turned to Maya. "How long do we have?"

"Based on current trends? Three to four months before the effects become widely visible. But small businesses are already feeling it." Maya thought of Mr. Lee and other restaurant suppliers. "Some are adapting. Others..."

Her phone buzzed – a text from her mother: "Urgent. Uncle Tuan's restaurant might close. Can you come home early?"

Maya looked up at Ms. Rodriguez, who nodded understanding. "Go. But I want a full report tomorrow. This changes everything."

At Phở Ngon, Maya found her parents talking with Uncle Tuan – not really her uncle, but her father's oldest friend and owner of another Vietnamese restaurant across town.

"His supplier doubled prices with no warning," her father explained. "Same happened to three other restaurants in the Asian district."

Maya opened her laptop. "Uncle Tuan, can I see your supplier contracts?"

As she reviewed his documents, her mind raced. The pattern was playing out exactly as her data predicted – but faster than expected.

"Here's what's happening," she explained in Vietnamese, pulling up her market analysis. "Traditional supply chains are breaking down. But that means we can build new ones."

She outlined her idea: a cooperative of local Asian restaurants and grocers, pooling resources and creating direct relationships with overseas suppliers. "Like the contract we negotiated with Mr. Lee, but bigger."

Her phone buzzed again – messages from her study group:

Tommy: "More theater departments want to join our supply co-op!"
Zoe: "Band parents association asking about your fundraising strategies."
Jessica: "Can your market analysis thing help orchestra budget too?"

Maya looked at the messages, then at her laptop showing the market projections, then at Uncle Tuan's worried face. Suddenly, she saw how it all connected.

"Uncle Tuan," she said, "what if this isn't just about saving your restaurant? What if we could help all the small businesses in the community?"

She quickly outlined her broader vision: using the same principles from her Nexus analysis to help local businesses adapt to the changing market. The restaurant cooperative could be just the beginning.

"But how?" Uncle Tuan asked. "We're just small restaurant owners."

"Not anymore," Maya's father said, looking proudly at his daughter. "Now we're part of something bigger."

Maya's phone lit up with an email from Ms. Rodriguez: "Board wants emergency meeting tomorrow. Bring full analysis and recommendation for strategy adjustment."

She looked around the restaurant – at her parents, at Uncle Tuan, at the laptop showing both global market patterns and local business data. The music metaphor had never felt more appropriate: old harmonies breaking down, new ones forming.

Tomorrow she would show the Nexus board how everything connected, from global supply chains to local restaurants to school theater departments. She would explain how small adaptations could create larger changes, how new networks were forming from the bottom up.

But tonight, she had AP Econ homework to finish. They were covering market disruption theory, and for once, Maya had more real-world examples than she could fit in her class notes.

"Maya," her mother called from the kitchen, "help me calculate new menu prices?"

"Coming!" Maya saved her work and closed her laptop. She had a feeling the next few months would bring more changes than anyone expected.

But maybe that wasn't a bad thing. After all, every great symphony needed moments of dissonance before finding its new harmony.

Chapter 10: Building New Harmonies

"You want us to bet our entire investment strategy on a theory developed by a high school intern?"

Maya kept her expression neutral as the Nexus board member continued his critique. She stood before the emergency board meeting, her data displayed on the screen behind her.

"With all due respect, sir," Maya replied, "I'm not asking you to bet on a theory. I'm showing you what's already happening." She clicked to her next slide. "These changes in supply chain dynamics are affecting businesses at every level. The question isn't whether to respond — it's how quickly we adapt."

Ms. Rodriguez leaned forward. "Walk us through the recommended strategy again."

Maya took a deep breath, remembering what Jessica always said before orchestra solos: "Trust your practice." She pulled up her market symphony visualization.

"Traditional supply chains are like an orchestra playing a familiar piece. Everyone knows their part, follows established patterns. But what we're seeing now..." She adjusted the musical visualization, letting them hear how the harmonies were shifting. "The music is changing. New players are entering, old relationships are breaking down, and new networks are forming."

She showed how small businesses were already creating alternative supply networks, how technology was enabling direct producer-consumer connections, how the old hierarchical distribution systems were fragmenting into more flexible networks.

"We have three options," Maya continued. "We can ignore these changes and maintain current investment strategies. We can fight against them by trying to prop up traditional supply chains. Or—" she switched to her final slides "—we can position ourselves to benefit from and support these emerging networks."

The skeptical board member scoffed. "And you're basing this on what? Restaurant supplies and school theater props?"

"Partially, yes," Maya acknowledged. "Because small businesses and local organizations are where you see these changes first. They're like the first violins in an orchestra – they show you where the music is going before the full symphony follows."

She pulled up her correlation data. "But I'm also basing it on these market indicators, these shipping patterns, and these emerging trade relationships. Everything points to the same conclusion: the market is reorganizing from the bottom up."

The room was quiet for a moment. Then the Goldman Sachs representative spoke up. "She's right. We're seeing similar patterns in other markets. Most analysts are missing it because they're looking at traditional indicators. But if you look at the aggregate data from small and medium businesses..."

The discussion that followed was intense, technical, and exactly what Maya had prepared for. By the end, even the skeptical board member was taking notes on her implementation strategy.

After the meeting, Maya rushed to her next challenge: a gathering of local restaurant owners at Phở Ngon. Her parents had convinced twelve other family-owned Asian restaurants to hear her cooperative proposal.

She arrived to find the restaurant's dining room filled with familiar faces — owners she'd known since childhood, who'd watched her grow up between the tables of their establishments.

"The same forces disrupting global supply chains are affecting us here," Maya explained, this time in a mixture of Vietnamese, Mandarin, and English. "But we can use these changes to our advantage."

She outlined her plan for a restaurant cooperative, showing how combined purchasing power could help them negotiate better prices and create direct relationships with overseas suppliers. She'd even created a simple app to help coordinate orders and share resources.

"Maya," Uncle Tuan interrupted, "we're simple restaurant owners. All this talk of market forces and supply chains..."

"Is affecting your businesses whether you understand it or not," Maya finished gently. "But look — I made these charts simpler..."

She walked them through the practical benefits: bulk ordering discounts, shared storage costs, coordinated deliveries. She'd calculated potential savings of 20-30% on key ingredients.

Her phone buzzed partway through – a message from Tommy: "Theater co-op works! First joint supply order saved us $2000!"

Maya smiled, adding that example to her presentation. By the end, ten of the twelve restaurants had agreed to join the cooperative's pilot program.

As the owners left, her father pulled her aside. "Your mother and I are proud of you. But Maya..." He looked concerned. "Don't forget to also be seventeen."

"Dad..."

"I mean it. You're doing amazing things, but don't miss your life while saving ours."

As if on cue, her phone lit up with messages from her friends:

Zoe: "HELLO? Dress rehearsal tomorrow? First chair needs her page turner!"
Tommy: "Cast party planning meeting! Your economic brain is required for pizza optimization."
Jessica: "Learning that Tchaikovsky piece you like. Practice together?"

Maya looked at her father. "Don't worry. I won't forget."

Later that evening, Maya sat in the school auditorium, turning pages for Zoe during band rehearsal while simultaneously running numbers on her laptop for both Nexus and the restaurant cooperative. The music washed over her as she worked – a complex piece with multiple movements.

She thought about how her analysis of market changes was like this music: different parts moving independently but ultimately working together to create something new. The challenge wasn't just understanding the changes, but helping others adapt to them.

Her phone buzzed with an email from Ms. Rodriguez: "Board approved your strategy. Implementation team meeting tomorrow. Also, Goldman Sachs expressed interest in summer internship."

Another message popped up, this time from Mr. Lee, the grocery supplier: "Other suppliers asking about your cooperative idea. Can we meet?"

And another from her mother: "Uncle Tuan's nephew wants app help for cooperative."

Maya looked up from her phone to see Zoe giving her a pointed look – she'd missed a page turn. "Sorry!" she whispered, quickly flipping the sheet music.

"Earth to Maya," Zoe whispered back during a rest. "You're doing that economics thing again, aren't you? That thing where you see patterns everywhere?"

"Maybe," Maya admitted. "But the patterns are leading to solutions. Look—" She started to pull up a chart, but Zoe stopped her.

"After practice. Right now, just listen to the music."

Maya nodded, closing her laptop. Her friend was right. Sometimes you needed to stop analyzing and just appreciate the symphony – even as it changed into something new.

Besides, she had a feeling the next few weeks would be intense enough. Between implementing changes at Nexus, launching the restaurant cooperative, and helping her friends with their spring performances, she would need all the mental rest she could get.

The band hit a crescendo, and Maya turned the page right on cue. Tomorrow would bring more challenges, more changes, more opportunities to help others adapt to the shifting economic landscape.

But tonight, she was just a teenager, turning pages for her friend, thinking about pizza party planning, and letting the music remind her that even the biggest changes could create beautiful harmonies – if you knew how to help them come together.

Chapter 11: Complex Rhythms

"No, no, the delivery schedule has to sync with everyone's prep times," Maya explained, pacing her bedroom with her phone pressed to her ear. It was 6 AM, and she was trying to coordinate the restaurant cooperative's first major supply order. "Uncle Tuan, tell Mrs. Liu that if she shifts her noodle prep to Tuesdays..."

A notification popped up on her laptop: urgent message from Marcus about the Nexus implementation strategy. Then another from Tommy: "CRISIS. Set pieces arriving today. Need your coordination magic!"

Maya flopped onto her bed, staring at the ceiling. She'd known implementing all these changes wouldn't be easy, but she hadn't expected every solution to create three new problems.

"Maya!" her mother called from downstairs. "You'll be late for school!"

Right. AP Physics test first period.

At school, Maya slid into her seat just as the bell rang. As Mr. Chen distributed the physics exams, she felt her phone vibrate: Mrs. Liu had messaged the cooperative's group chat about delivery conflicts.

"Phones away," Mr. Chen reminded the class.

Maya tucked her phone into her bag, trying to focus on acceleration and force vectors. But her mind kept drifting to other vectors — market forces, supply chain dynamics, the delicate balance of coordinating multiple restaurants' needs...

"Ten minutes left," Mr. Chen announced.

Maya blinked at her half-completed test. Physics would have to take a backseat to economics today. She rushed through the remaining problems, hoping her answers made sense.

Between classes, she found Tommy waiting by her locker, wringing his hands.

"The set pieces are great, and the bulk ordering saved us a ton of money," he said, "but now three schools want them delivered on the same day, and the supplier only has one truck, and—"

"Breathe," Maya interrupted, pulling out her laptop. "This is just another logistics problem. Like restaurant deliveries, but with bigger pieces."

She quickly created a delivery optimization model, similar to the one she'd made for the restaurant cooperative. "See? If we stagger the deliveries and have schools within five miles of each other share trucks..."

"You're a lifesaver," Tommy sighed. Then he peered at her more closely. "Have you slept?"

"Sleep is for people who don't have to revolutionize supply chains," Maya joked. But truth be told, she was exhausted.

In AP Econ, Mr. Washington was discussing market efficiency. For once, Maya wasn't raising her hand every five minutes – she was too busy trying to subtly check messages from both the cooperative and Nexus under her desk.

"Maya?" Mr. Washington called. "You're usually eager to share real-world examples. Any thoughts on how market efficiency applies to current events?"

Maya looked up, her mind spinning with everything she was juggling. Then she had an idea.

"Actually, yes." She stood up, suddenly energized. "What we're learning about market efficiency doesn't fully account for emerging network effects in supply chains. Traditional models assume..."

She launched into an explanation of what she'd been seeing with both the restaurant cooperative and the theater supply network. Mr. Washington looked increasingly intrigued.

"That's... a fascinating analysis," he said when she finished. "And you're seeing this in real-world applications?"

"I'm kind of living it," Maya admitted.

After class, Mr. Washington asked her to stay behind. "Maya, your understanding of economics has grown exponentially. But..." He gestured at the physics test sticking out of her bag, a 'C' visible on the corner. "Don't let one passion come at the expense of everything else."

Maya nodded, thinking of her father's similar warning. But how could she step back when so many people were counting on her?

At lunch, she found Zoe and Jessica at their usual table. She opened her laptop, ready to work, but Zoe closed it firmly.

"Nope. Friend time. No economics for at least twenty minutes."

"But—"

"The cooperative can wait," Jessica added. "Tell us about you. How are you doing with all this?"

Maya hesitated. How was she doing? Between coordinating the cooperative, implementing strategies at Nexus, helping with school activities, maintaining her grades (mostly), and still working at her parents' restaurant...

"I'm fine," she started to say, but Zoe's skeptical look stopped her. "Okay, maybe a little overwhelmed. It's just... everyone needs everything now, and every solution seems to create new problems, and—"

"Sounds like that piece we're learning in orchestra," Jessica mused. "You know, the one with all the competing rhythms that somehow have to work together?"

Maya perked up. "That's it! That's exactly what this is like! All these different patterns that seem conflicting but actually—"

"Ah ah!" Zoe interrupted. "No turning this into an economics metaphor. Twenty minutes of normal teenage lunch conversation."

Maya laughed, realizing how much she needed this. They talked about Jessica's college audition preparations, Zoe's latest band drama, and Tommy's theatrical crisis of confidence about playing Mark in "Rent."

But her phone kept buzzing: cooperative members with questions, Nexus colleagues seeking input, her mother asking about afternoon prep schedules...

"Okay," Zoe said finally, "release the economics kraken. But Maya? Remember to breathe between movements."

Maya smiled at the musical metaphor as she opened her laptop. Her friends were right — she needed to find a better rhythm, a way to balance all these competing demands.

She opened her coordination app, then stopped. What if the problem wasn't just about scheduling? What if, like in orchestra, the solution was helping everyone hear how their parts fit together?

"I need to make some changes to the app," she muttered, fingers flying across the keyboard. "Make it more collaborative, let everyone see the whole picture..."

Her phone buzzed again — Ms. Rodriguez wanted to discuss implementation challenges. Then another message from Uncle Tuan about supplier negotiations. Then Tommy about set delivery coordination.

Maya took a deep breath, remembering Jessica's performance advice: focus on one measure at a time, but never lose sight of the larger piece.

She could do this. She just needed to help everyone find their rhythm in this new economic symphony she'd helped start.

But first, maybe she should apologize to Mr. Chen about that physics test.

Looking at her friends, at her buzzing phone, at the complex schedules on her screen, Maya realized something: the hardest part of changing economic systems wasn't the economics – it was helping people adapt to new rhythms while keeping the music playing.

Good thing she had experience turning pages in orchestra. This was just a bigger, more complex score.

And somehow, she'd help everyone learn to play it together.

Chapter 12: Delegation and Harmony

"What if we taught the app to more people?" Maya's mother suggested over breakfast, watching her daughter simultaneously eat cereal, check supplier messages, and review Nexus data.

Maya looked up, a spoonful of Cheerios halfway to her mouth. "What do you mean?"

"Uncle Tuan's nephew is good with computers. Mrs. Liu's daughter is studying business at UTD. Why do you have to coordinate everything yourself?"

The question hit Maya like a revelation. She'd been so focused on creating solutions that she'd forgotten about something crucial: building capacity in others.

At school, she found her friends in their usual morning spots – Tommy rehearsing lines while checking theater budgets, Zoe organizing band fundraiser details, Jessica reviewing orchestra scores.

"I need your help," Maya announced. "All of you."

She explained her idea: instead of trying to manage everything herself, she could teach others to use the systems she'd created. The restaurant cooperative could have a team of coordinators, the theater supply network could have representatives at each school, and she could delegate some of her Nexus analysis to her research team.

"Like sections in an orchestra," Jessica observed. "Each part knowing its role but understanding how it fits into the whole."

"Exactly!" Maya pulled out her laptop. "Look, I've already started modifying the apps to be more user-friendly..."

In AP Econ, Mr. Washington was discussing organizational economics and management theory. For once, Maya wasn't distracted by constant messages – she'd scheduled a proper training session for the cooperative members that afternoon.

"The most efficient organizations," Mr. Washington explained, "aren't necessarily the most centralized. Sometimes, distributed networks can respond more effectively to change."

Maya smiled, thinking of her new approach. She raised her hand. "Like how companies are moving away from traditional hierarchies toward more collaborative structures?"

"Precisely. Can you elaborate?"

Maya shared how she'd seen this principle working in both small businesses and larger corporations, carefully avoiding specific mentions of the cooperative or Nexus. Her classmates actually seemed interested – especially when she connected it to things they understood, like social media networks and music streaming platforms.

After class, she headed to Nexus, where she had a new proposal for her research team.

"We've been approaching this implementation from the top down," she told them. "But what if we reversed it? Let the people closest to each market segment take the lead?"

Marcus leaned back in his chair, intrigued. "Go on."

Maya showed how they could create specialized teams for different aspects of the market transition, each sharing insights with the others. "Like different instruments in a symphony, each with their own expertise but working together."

"There's that music metaphor again," Marcus smiled. "But it makes sense. We've been trying to conduct everything from above, when we should be enabling each section to play its part."

That afternoon, Maya hosted the first training session for the restaurant cooperative at Phở Ngon. She'd created simple tutorials, translated into multiple languages, showing how to use the coordination app and understand basic market indicators.

Uncle Tuan's nephew, David, picked up the technical aspects quickly. Mrs. Liu's daughter, Jennifer, immediately saw ways to improve the business analytics. Soon, they were suggesting enhancements Maya hadn't even considered.

"See?" her mother said, bringing out drinks for everyone. "Many hands make light work."

Maya watched as the restaurant owners began teaching each other different aspects of the system. Mr. Lee, their original supplier, was explaining supply chain logistics to newer cooperative members. Mrs. Liu was showing others how to optimize their ordering patterns.

Her phone buzzed – but instead of the usual flood of questions, it was Tommy sharing good news: "Other schools' drama departments love the delegate system! Each school now has a supply coordinator. PS: You're still coming to rehearsal, right? We need our economic advisor for the 'La Vie Bohème' staging."

Then a message from Ms. Rodriguez: "Your distributed implementation strategy is working. Board wants to expand it to other divisions."

Maya smiled, finally feeling like she could breathe. She opened her physics textbook – she had a makeup test tomorrow, and this time she intended to ace it.

Jessica slid into the booth across from her, violin case in tow. "Ready to actually practice that Tchaikovsky piece? No economics talk allowed."

"Actually, yes," Maya realized. By sharing the load with others, she could reclaim some time for herself.

That evening, after a productive orchestra practice, Maya sat with her parents during the restaurant's quiet period. She showed them how the cooperative members were already taking initiative, solving problems without her constant intervention.

"You're learning one of the most important lessons in business," her father said. "Success isn't about doing everything yourself – it's about helping others succeed too."

Maya nodded, watching through the window as the Dallas sunset painted the sky in brilliant colors. Her phone buzzed with updates: cooperative members helping each other with deliveries, theater departments coordinating set piece sharing, her research team at Nexus making new discoveries.

The systems she'd created were starting to run themselves, guided by the people who used them every day. Like an orchestra that didn't need constant conducting once everyone knew their parts.

She turned back to her physics notes, feeling more balanced than she had in weeks. Tomorrow would bring new challenges, but she no longer had to face them alone.

Her mother set a fresh cup of Vietnamese coffee beside her textbook. "Now that you're not trying to solve everyone's problems by yourself, maybe you can help me plan next month's menu?"

"Actually," Maya said, "I think Mrs. Liu's daughter had some great ideas about menu optimization. Want me to connect you two?"

Her mother laughed. "Look at you, still connecting people and markets, just more efficiently now."

Maya grinned, turning back to her physics. She'd finally learned something that wasn't in any economics textbook: the best solutions often came from empowering others to solve their own problems.

Through the restaurant's windows, she could see the lights of downtown Dallas, where tomorrow she'd share her latest insights with the Nexus team. But tonight, she was just a teenager doing homework in her family's restaurant, surrounded by the community she'd helped bring together.

And for once, that felt like exactly enough.

Chapter 13: Testing the Symphony

"The cooperative saved us nearly forty percent on our bulk order this month," Mrs. Liu announced during their weekly meeting at Phở Ngon. "And Jennifer's menu optimization suggestions increased our profits by fifteen percent!"

Maya sat back, contentedly sipping her mother's coffee as she watched the restaurant owners share their successes. The cooperative was running smoothly now, with different members taking lead roles in coordination, technology, and supplier negotiations.

Her phone buzzed – a message from Ms. Rodriguez: "Need you in the office ASAP. Major market shift detected."

Maya's contentment evaporated. She quickly said goodbye to the cooperative members and headed downtown, her mind racing. Had she missed something in her analysis?

At Nexus, she found Marcus and Ms. Rodriguez studying a wall of red-tinged market indicators.

"Remember how you predicted the supply chain reorganization?" Marcus asked. "Well, it's happening faster than anyone expected. And it's causing some... unexpected reactions."

Maya looked at the data and felt her stomach drop. Large traditional suppliers, seeing their market share threatened by new cooperative networks, were slashing prices to levels that smaller networks couldn't match.

"They're trying to crush the emerging networks before they can establish themselves," Maya realized. "Like a price war, but targeted specifically at cooperative structures."

"Your restaurant cooperative and theater supply network could be affected," Ms. Rodriguez said gently. "Along with thousands of similar organizations nationwide."

Maya's phone lit up with messages:

Tommy: "Emergency! Supplier canceled our joint order. Says they have a 'new pricing structure.'"
David (Uncle Tuan's nephew): "Big suppliers offering individual restaurants 60% discounts to leave cooperative???"
Jennifer (Mrs. Liu's daughter): "Need your help analyzing these new market pressures!"

Maya took a deep breath, remembering what she'd learned about delegation and collaboration. "Let me call a few people."

She set up an emergency video conference, connecting her Nexus research team with key members of both the restaurant cooperative and the theater supply network. As everyone joined, she could see the worry on their faces.

"What we're facing isn't just a price war," Maya explained, sharing her screen. "It's a fundamental battle between old and new market structures. But remember what we learned about network effects?"

She pulled up her symphony visualization, but now added new elements. "Traditional suppliers have scale, but we have flexibility. They're playing one loud instrument, trying to drown out the rest. We're an orchestra – many parts working together."

"But how can we compete with their prices?" Uncle Tuan asked.

"We don't compete directly," Maya said. "We adapt. Jennifer, remember that analysis you did on variable costs? David, your work on delivery optimization? We can use those insights to..."

For the next hour, they brainstormed solutions, each person contributing their expertise. The Nexus team provided market analysis, the restaurant owners shared practical insights, and the theater coordinators offered creative approaches to resource sharing.

"What if we expanded our networks?" Jennifer suggested. "Connect with other cooperatives nationwide?"

"Create a meta-network," Maya mused, excitement building. "Share resources, information, and bargaining power across multiple cooperatives..."

She quickly modeled the potential impact, using her musical market visualization to show how different networks could harmonize their efforts.

"It's like a musical fugue," Jessica commented from the theater group call. "Each part enters independently but contributes to a larger pattern."

"Exactly!" Maya turned to Ms. Rodriguez. "This is bigger than just defending against price cutting. It's an opportunity to demonstrate the real strength of networked economics."

Ms. Rodriguez was already nodding. "How fast can we implement?"

"With everyone working together? Days, not weeks."

The next few days were intense but different from Maya's earlier overwhelming experiences. Instead of trying to manage everything herself, she focused on coordinating the various teams' efforts.

The restaurant cooperative members reached out to other Asian restaurant associations across Texas. The theater departments connected with schools in other states. The Nexus team helped analyze and optimize these expanding networks.

By week's end, they had created something remarkable: a resilient network of networks, each maintaining local autonomy while benefiting from shared resources and information.

"It's beautiful," Marcus said, watching Maya's visualization of the interconnected systems. "Like a symphony orchestra that spans the country."

Maya smiled, thinking of how far they'd come from her first attempts to help her parents' restaurant. "The best part is, it's self-sustaining now. Each node in the network makes the whole system stronger."

Her phone buzzed – Tommy sharing photos from "Rent" rehearsal: "Set pieces arrived through the new network! Better quality than before, AND cheaper!"

Then messages from the cooperative: multiple restaurants reporting their best month ever, despite the market pressures.

That evening, Maya sat in orchestra practice, actually focusing on the music instead of running numbers in her head. The Tchaikovsky piece they were playing seemed particularly appropriate – complex, challenging, but ultimately harmonious.

"You seem calmer," Jessica noted during a break. "Even with everything that's happening."

"Because I'm not trying to control everything anymore," Maya replied. "I'm just helping each part find its place in the larger piece."

Her phone lit up with an email from Goldman Sachs: they weren't just interested in a summer internship anymore – they wanted to study the cooperative network model for potential broader applications.

Maya smiled, turning back to her sheet music. She'd learned something profound about both economics and life: the most powerful systems weren't controlled from above but grew from countless independent parts working in harmony.

Just then, another message arrived – her mother, reminding her about dinner prep. Because even with all the economic innovations and market transformations, some things remained delightfully constant.

And that too was part of the symphony.

Chapter 14: Opening Night

"Maya, you need to see this."

Maya looked up from her AP Economics homework to find Tommy practically bouncing with excitement in the school library. He turned his laptop toward her, showing a news article:

"SMALL BUSINESS REVOLUTION: New Cooperative Networks Challenge Traditional Supply Chains"

The article detailed how restaurant cooperatives and school theater departments across the country were forming interconnected networks, creating unprecedented bargaining power and efficiency for small organizations. It even mentioned the Dallas Asian Restaurant Cooperative as one of the pioneering models.

"We're trending on Twitter," Tommy grinned. "#SmallBizNetwork and #CoopPower are going viral."

Maya's phone buzzed – Ms. Rodriguez sharing similar articles from Bloomberg and The Wall Street Journal. The financial press was calling it a "grassroots economic transformation."

"Don't forget about tonight," Tommy added, closing his laptop. "'Rent' opens at 7:00. The theater's already sold out – turns out our new pricing strategy worked too well."

Right. Opening night. In all the excitement about the cooperative networks, Maya had almost forgotten about the school performances that had helped inspire her economic innovations.

"I'll be there," she promised. "Front row, stage left, just like always."

But first, she had meetings at both Nexus and the restaurant cooperative. The network expansion had exceeded everyone's expectations, and now they needed to manage the growth sustainably.

At Nexus, Maya found her research team excitedly analyzing data from across the country.

"Look at these adoption rates," Marcus said, pointing to a chart. "Other industries are starting to copy the model. There's a network of independent bookstores in Seattle, craft breweries in Portland, even family farms in the Midwest..."

Maya pulled up her symphony visualization, now significantly more complex than her original version. "Each new network adds its own voice to the piece," she explained, letting them hear how the different sectors created new harmonies in the market data.

"Goldman Sachs called again," Ms. Rodriguez mentioned casually. "They're creating a new division focused on cooperative network financing. They want you to consult... after you finish high school, of course."

Maya grinned. A year ago, she'd been worried about helping her parents' restaurant survive. Now she was shaping national economic policy. Speaking of which...

At the cooperative meeting, held in Phở Ngon's newly expanded dining room, Maya watched proudly as Jennifer and David led the discussion. They'd taken her basic coordination app and improved it dramatically, adding features she hadn't even considered.

"We're getting calls from restaurant associations in Houston, Austin, even California," Jennifer reported. "Everyone wants to know how we made this work."

"Tell them the truth," Maya's father spoke up. "It worked because we stopped competing and started cooperating. Like Maya's orchestra – everyone playing their own part but creating something bigger together."

Maya checked her phone – messages from Zoe and Jessica about the evening's performances. The spring musical would be followed by a combined band and orchestra concert, showcasing the arts programs they'd helped save through economic innovation.

"Maya," her mother called from the kitchen. "Help me with the special opening night menu?"

They'd created a pre-theater dinner service, coordinating with other restaurants in the cooperative to handle the increased demand. The combination of optimized pricing, shared resources, and coordinated scheduling had turned potential competition into mutual benefit.

As Maya helped prep ingredients, her mother hummed along with the Vietnamese pop music playing in the kitchen. "Remember when you first asked to see the restaurant's books?"

"Seems like a lifetime ago," Maya replied, expertly slicing green onions.

"You've helped so many people." Her mother touched her cheek. "But don't forget to enjoy your own success too."

That evening, Maya sat in the school auditorium, watching Tommy and the cast perform "Rent." The set pieces acquired through their supply network looked professional under the stage lights. The program listed all the school theater departments that had joined their cooperative, now spanning three states.

During intermission, she checked her phone to find more messages about the expanding economic networks. But for once, she didn't feel compelled to respond immediately. Tonight was about celebrating what these innovations had helped create – not just successful businesses, but thriving communities.

The second act began, and Maya watched as her classmates performed "La Vie Bohème," a song about artists building community in the face of economic pressure. How appropriate, she thought, that their own economic innovation had started with trying to save the arts.

After the show, during the standing ovation, Maya felt tears in her eyes. Part of it was pride in her friends' performance, but it was more than that. She was witnessing the real-world impact of economic theories she'd learned in AP class – how markets could be shaped to help people, not just generate profits.

"Ready for the concert?" Jessica asked, finding her after the show. She was already in her orchestra uniform.

Maya nodded, following her friend backstage. Through the stage door, she could hear the band warming up, Zoe's French horn rising above the general cacophony.

Her phone buzzed one last time – an email from Mr. Washington, her AP Econ teacher: "Just read about your cooperative networks in the Journal. This is why we study economics – to make real change. PS: Looking forward to your presentation on network theory tomorrow."

Maya smiled, tucking her phone away. The band was starting, the orchestra would follow, and somewhere in the music of markets and melodies, she'd helped create something new.

Tomorrow would bring more challenges, more opportunities, more chances to help others understand how economics could work for everyone. But tonight was for celebrating how far they'd come – with a symphony of success played by many hands working in harmony.

The conductor raised his baton, and Maya settled in to simply listen, knowing that sometimes the most beautiful music came from letting everyone play their part.

Chapter 15: Full Symphony

Maya stood at the podium in the Dallas Convention Center, looking out at a sea of faces. The "Small Business Network Summit" had drawn hundreds of participants from across the country – restaurant owners, theater directors, suppliers, economists, and even a few AP Economics teachers, including Mr. Washington, who sat beaming in the front row.

"Six months ago," Maya began, "I was just trying to help my parents' restaurant survive rising costs. I never imagined that understanding supply and demand curves would lead to..." She gestured at the crowded hall. "All of this."

The presentation screen behind her showed her now-famous market symphony visualization, evolved far beyond its original form. Different colored lights represented thousands of small businesses, their connections forming intricate patterns that moved like musical notes across the display.

"Economic theories aren't just abstract concepts in textbooks," she continued. "They're tools for understanding how we can work together to create something bigger than ourselves. Like an orchestra, where every instrument matters, every business in our network contributes to the greater whole."

In the audience, she spotted her parents sitting with Uncle Tuan and Mrs. Liu. The restaurant cooperative had grown to include over fifty establishments across Texas, with similar networks sprouting up nationwide. Phở Ngon was having its best year ever, and more importantly, the whole community was thriving.

"The old model of competition isn't the only way," Maya explained, switching to her data slides. "When we share resources, information, and opportunities, we all benefit. The mathematics of network effects proves it." She highlighted key statistics showing how cooperative members consistently outperformed traditional businesses across multiple metrics.

Her phone buzzed quietly – probably Tommy sharing photos from the final performance of "Rent," which had enjoyed a record-breaking run thanks to their optimized pricing strategy. The theater supply network now connected drama departments in five states, making ambitious productions possible for schools that could never have afforded them before.

"But the real success isn't in the numbers," Maya said, clicking to her final slides. "It's in the stories." She showed pictures: restaurant owners helping each other during busy times, school theaters sharing resources, suppliers working directly with small business networks.

"When I started my internship at Nexus Analytics, I thought economics was all about maximizing profits. What I learned instead was that true economic value comes from maximizing connections."

In the second row, Ms. Rodriguez and Marcus nodded approvingly. Nexus had implemented Maya's network analysis across all its divisions, and their new cooperative business unit was revolutionizing how Wall Street thought about small business investment.

"The AP Economics curriculum taught me about market forces," Maya acknowledged, smiling at Mr. Washington. "But you all taught me how to use those forces to help people. Every small business owner who joined our network, every student who helped coordinate resources, every supplier who took a chance on a new way of doing things — you're all part of this economic symphony."

The visualization behind her shifted to show the real-time status of their national network. Thousands of points of light pulsed in harmony, each representing a business or organization connected to the whole.

"And we're just getting started," Maya continued. "The cooperative model is spreading to new industries every day. Independent bookstores, family farms, craft manufacturers — all discovering that they're stronger together than apart."

She glanced at her parents again, remembering those early morning conversations over restaurant prep, when understanding economics seemed like a matter of survival. Now it was about something much bigger: showing how markets could work for everyone.

"Next fall, I'll be starting college," Maya announced. "I've accepted a scholarship to study Economics and Data Science at MIT." A proud smile from her parents. "But I'll still be working with our networks, still helping to grow these connections. Because what we've built together is more than just a business model — it's a community model."

Her phone buzzed again — messages from Zoe and Jessica this time. They were setting up for the evening's special performance: a combined concert featuring school music programs from across their network, celebrating how their economic innovation had helped save and strengthen arts education.

"Tonight, you'll hear an actual symphony," Maya said, wrapping up her speech. "Students from twenty schools, playing together. A year ago, many of their programs were struggling with budget cuts. Now they're thriving, thanks to the same principles that helped our businesses: cooperation, coordination, and understanding how individual parts create a greater whole."

The audience rose in applause, but Maya wasn't finished. "And if you listen carefully to their music, you might hear something familiar – the sound of many different voices coming together to create something beautiful. Just like our economic network."

The applause grew louder. Maya saw Mrs. Liu wiping away tears, Uncle Tuan grinning broadly, her parents holding hands proudly. Mr. Washington was nodding enthusiastically while scribbling notes – probably already planning how to incorporate this into next year's AP Econ lessons.

Later that evening, Maya sat in the auditorium as hundreds of student musicians filed onto the stage. She spotted Zoe with her French horn, Jessica with her violin, all part of this greater symphony they'd helped make possible.

Her phone had more messages: Tommy sharing cast photos, Jennifer reporting new cooperative statistics, Marcus sending market analyses. But they could wait. Right now, she wanted to simply listen as the music began.

The conductor raised his baton, and Maya closed her eyes as the first notes filled the hall. In the harmony of strings and brass and woodwinds, she heard an echo of her market visualization — many individual parts working together to create something greater than the sum of their parts.

She thought about everything that had happened since that first interview at Nexus: the challenges she'd faced, the solutions she'd found, the people she'd helped, the lessons she'd learned. Economics wasn't just about money — it was about understanding connections, about helping people work together better.

The music swelled, and Maya Chen — daughter, student, innovator, and now recognized economic pioneer — smiled. She'd started by trying to understand supply and demand, and ended up helping create a whole new way of thinking about markets and community.

As the symphony played on, Maya opened her notebook and began sketching ideas for the next phase of their network. Because this wasn't an ending — it was just the beginning of a whole new movement in their economic symphony.

And she couldn't wait to hear what they would create together next.

About the Author

Brandon T. Mayes M.Ed. is an educator, husband, father, foodie, author, and entrepreneur. After being in the classroom for over a decade, he noticed that students needed a 'novel' way to gain new information. Adding his love of education, reading, and the world, he has embarked on a journey to make economics engaging.